THE RUG

J H BARTLETT

outskirts
press

One

"I picture myself in a few years barely able to get out the door, the house covered in vines and wild roses, the shingles falling off, the roof leaking and the children trying to put me in a nursing home. I've given up weeding. Uninvited plants have sprouted up and are taking over as never before. I like them better than the ones I've planted, anyway. How are things with you?"

"That's why I'm calling." Parker replied. "Priscilla's in pretty bad shape and I'm told she needs to go into what they insist upon calling assisted living. "

"No . . . I knew she was getting a little forgetful but I had a no idea. I'm sorry to hear this. Have you made any plans—is there a good place up there?"

"We're moving back to Massachusetts, in fact to Plymouth. I've made reservations for her at a place on Pilgrim Road. All the children are in the Boston area. We have no close family here in Ontario. Do you think there's room for me there at in the compound? Actually, Dottie, I'd like to move into the Guest House with you."

"Are you crazy? Don't be ridiculous."

"I'm not proposing marriage or even sleeping together. But you know we get along well. Remember, it was almost me and you instead of Paul and you. "

"Your brother is barely in the ground. Pricilla's still alive. We're pushing eighty. This is totally unacceptable. Practically incestuous."

"Okay. Forget it. I'll figure something out after I get Priscilla settled. Rent a condo somewhere downtown maybe. Just thought I could help with some of the bills. How much are you paying in taxes this year?"

"Never mind about my finances. It's none of your damn business How close are you to making the move?"

"I've signed her up at Ocean View Acres starting next month. She's declining fast. Someone suggested I get in touch with a guy called Loring Crankshaw to help with the move. Ever hear of him? He's from Boston. Son of a fairly well-known painter. Comes highly recommended. I have no idea how to even begin with a move like this. He apparently has a lot of experience, knows the right people to call, what to throw out, what to sell, what to take and what to leave in the house. I'm hanging on to the house here. Good to have a bolt hole in Canada these days. The kids are threatening to emigrate."

"Let me get back to you Parker. My cousin Sue's husband, Ted, mentioned something about Crankshaw."

When he landed in Plymouth after his retirement, Ted Bumblechock was asked to help out in town government. There was an opening coming up on the Planning Board and Ted's experience in government and his background in city planning was what was needed in this formerly quiet historic small town, all too quickly turning into a commute to Boston town. Ted was invited for dinner to meet some of the town's movers and shakers at Isaac and Charity Snodgrass's house in downtown Plymouth. Their family lines were firmly connected to many of the Mayflower passengers.

They were having drinks in the living room before dinner. "Interesting rug," Ted said to Isaac Snodgrass. "Looks like the one I used to play on at my Grandparents'."

"Yeah, we got it a few years ago. Seemed just right for this room. It's Persian, from Isfahan I believe. What new ideas are you bringing us from the great world outside of Plymouth on how to run this town?"

"Well, I'm still new here. I need to listen and learn what plans are afoot first." He was distracted. The rug.

"You will find it's not simple here in Plymouth. People have lots of ideas. Many opinions coming from many different backgrounds. It's a great town, but not cohesive."

"Where did you say you got the rug?"

"I have no idea. Better ask my wife."

Ted wandered through the crowd searching for Charity Snodgrass, chatting with others, gin and tonic in hand, walking over France, Germany, and Belgium. He had played war on this rug, or one just like it, at his grandmother's house in East Middleton. There were no toys in her house. Chessmen were his soldiers. White were the allies; black the axis powers.

The rug sat in the middle of his grandparents' living room in East Middleton. The only thing of beauty in their dark gloomy house with its heavy Victorian furniture, velvet curtains and damask covered chairs. Earlier the rug had been under the enormous oak dining room table. His grandfather had cut a hole in the rug for the toaster cord. The toaster was always on the dining room table: breakfast, lunch and dinner. It was the center piece, for some unfathomable reason. The cord ran from the toaster off the side of table through a hole cut in the rug to the electric outlet on the floor under the table

By the time Ted came along the rug had been moved to the living room to be replaced by one of lesser quality under the dining room table, which also had a hole cut in it for the toaster cord. The Isfahan covered most of the living room floor and became Ted's playground when his parents left him at his grandparent's house. Each design on the rug was part of the geography of Europe. The three large geometric designs in the center were Germany, France, and the Netherlands. The smaller designs beside and between were Italy, Belgium and the Baltic countries. Along the edges of the rug the geometric patterns framing the larger interior designs were rivers, forests, lakes. Ted always lined up the white chessmen on the Atlantic Ocean edge of France, the black chessmen headed toward the white, westward from Germany. He liked to keep the black king in the toaster cord hole. Hitler in his bunker.

Ted moved from group to group, a typical Plymouth cocktail party routine. Small talk, jokes, family stories. He was able to maneuver himself to Germany. He dropped the small paper cocktail napkin that came with his drink. As he squatted to pick it up, he felt around under the napkin. Yes! There was the hole, Hitler's bunker.

The next day, he called his cousin Nancy. "Do you know what happened to Grandma's living room rug? I believe we were sent a list of the family treasures when she died but I didn't pay much attention – we were out of the country."

"Well hello to you, too, Ted. How is your family and how are things in Plymouth? I thought you diplomats were supposed to be good at small talk. How about a little chat with your long lost cousin first, before demanding answers? It's been a long time."

They talked about friends and family and the sad state of the world. When there was a break, Nancy said, "Yeah, we all got the list of the family treasures when Grandma died and another one later when Aunt Harriet herself died and her condo was sold. That rug was not on either list. Maybe you never heard. Loring Crankshaw helped Aunt Harriet clean out and minimize the old house. Later he helped her move into her retirement apartment. He sold off Grandma's things that no one wanted. Rumor has it that he helped himself to some treasures along the way."

"Loring Crankshaw? You mean the son of Eliot Crankshaw, the artist?"

"That's the one. I remember how pleased we were that he could help as he did. We weren't at all sorry to see the lovely rooms he created for Aunt Harriet, not that she gave much of a damn. It was much later that we learned he sashayed through life living on his father's reputation, and bilking widows and relatives out of family treasures along the way.

"What happened to the things Aunt Harriet didn't take?"

"After we all had our pick of the stuff, he ran an auction at Grandma's house and afterward called in some local charity to take away what nobody wanted. When he finished at Aunt Harriet's he stayed on and slept in her spare room. He told her a job was opening for him in Virginia. 'If I could just stay on here with you for a few more weeks, I'll try not to be a burden to you, Miss Upchurch,' I heard him say."

"That's quite a story, Nancy. I'm pretty sure the rug from Grandma's living room is now here in Plymouth. I'm going to see if I can find out how it got here. And, I believe the Tappertits have taken on Loring Crankshaw to help Priscilla and Parker move down to Plymouth from Ontario. Priscilla has become, as they say 'a little forgetful' and has to go into a nursing home, and Parker figured it might as well be here in Plymouth as there. But Dorothy must know Crankshaw's story."

"I wouldn't know. Dorothy and I were never the best of friends. I didn't know Crankshaw was still in business, so to speak. Of course I haven't been in the market for his services, nor have my friends . . . not yet."

Ted told Dorothy about Crankshaw but not about the rug. He wanted to do a little more research about its provenance and not jump in and make accusations. He mentioned to Dorothy that Crankshaw had helped his family years ago. He was remembered as being very good at his work. Kind of a glorified decorator/consultant. Well worth having.

TWO

What is the first name of your maternal grandmother, the laptop asks if Ted forgets or confuses the secret pass word. ALICE he types. He doesn't forget her. He remembers all those times when he was left with his grandparents. He remembers the rugs, the small room where he slept with wallpaper of squirrels, the stone walls he played on, his grumpy grandfather. The rug was the only thing colorful in her drab dark living room with its dull brick fireplace, the wing chair covered in maroon velveteen, a stiff couch upholstered in green damask, wooden rocking chair next to the fireplace. The room was neat and clean but without joy, uncomfortable with no signs of games or books. She had a dachshund, ugly and bad tempered. It was only the vast colorful rug from Persia that held joy and happiness in that room. Now it is here in an old house in downtown Plymouth.

1946

In the evenings, after setting the table for the next morning's breakfast, Alice Appleby Upchurch would lay out her clothes for the following day on the wing chair in the living room, next to the radiator. At 7 a.m. each morning she would leave her large bed in the east chamber, and in dressing gown and slippers descend the front hall stairs to dress in her warmed up clothes. Seven year old Ted liked to sit on the footstool in front of the wing chair and watch his grandmother dress. First the brassiere, a large garment since she was well endowed, then the underpants (similar to boxer shorts, only in satin), then the girdle, the corset, the garter belt, the stockings. Next the slip and finally the dress, which, by comparison to what went under it, was disappointingly simple—some sort of a print with a matching belt for what was by then no longer a waist. Leather shoes with low heels and shoelaces. She arranged her hair into a bun held by tortoise shell hair pins under a hairnet. And finally the rimless glasses. It was a long and leisurely levee.

Grandpa Upchurch made his own

breakfast. Alice would leave the double boiler with water in the bottom on the cold stove the night before with the bag of oatmeal close by. He boiled two eggs in the bottom water while his oatmeal cooked in the top. Parsimonious and proud of it and of the money he was able put aside as a farmer. The dining room table held his single breakfast place setting: a linen placemat under his plate, coffee cup, saucer, silver spoon, knife and fork. The cord of the toaster ran off the side of the table to an electric outlet on the floor through a hole cut in the Oriental rug.

Leonard T. Mellodigian called at the house every week on Thursday to show rugs recently arrived from Persia, Iraq and Turkey. A charming man, a gentleman. Alice would wear her better dress on those days, apply a hint of rouge to her cheeks, a light coating of pink to her lips. Her hair was loosely arranged on Thursdays into more of a French twist than the usual tight farmer's wife bun. Mr. Mellodigian, after removing several rugs from his car and draping them around the house, accepted her offer of coffee, admired her broach and the lace at the neck of her dress. She blushed at his compliments. They were both aware that Thursday was the day her husband brought the boxes of carnations to market in Boston, a three hour round trip, sometimes four if he stopped to visit Elmira on the way home.

Alice ran her hands over each rug after Mr. Mellodigian had unrolled two or three. He stood close to her pointing out the beautiful design, the flawless stitching on the back.

"But no, no," he corrected himself and pointed his finger, his head now close to hers. "Not flawless," he corrected. "Never perfect. See this jagged place here . . . not quite perfect. Only God is perfect."

"Mmm," Alice hummed, thinking how interesting it was that he, from such a different world, could have the same philosophical views as hers.

Alice's grandfather, John Goodfellow, believed in women's education. He had put aside funds so that all of his granddaughters could go to boarding school and college. Most of them went to St. Cushnet Academy and then on to one of the "seven sisters". Alice went to Smith. Apparently Old John Goodfellow (as he is always called because he lived to be 101) didn't think a formal education was necessary for the boys. No education fund was set up for them. They could learn what they needed to know on the farm. But the girls were expected to become teachers and civic leaders and raise their children intelligently. Strong women threaded through the family for generations. Women who never felt the need for joining feminist activities. Alice descended from families who had come during the wave of Puritans arriving in Boston in the mid 1600's, shortly after the Pilgrims who arrived in Plymouth in 1620. From Boston, they had moved west to settle in Wayland, Sudbury, Middleton and further onward.

Alice's husband, Charles Morgan Upchurch was from Maine. In the early 1900's he came down from Aroostook County on the train each Friday with a load of potatoes going to market in Boston. His ancestors had been Royalists during the U.S. War of Independence and had left their Connecticut farm to move to New Brunswick. Later generations moved back to the U.S. to raise potatoes when things were quieter. One Friday, just after his 20th birthday, Charles saw an advertisement in the Boston Transcript for a job on a farm in Middleton. He went out from Boston by bus and was hired by John Appleby to help on his run-down dirt farm in East Middleton.

John Appleby had five sons and four daughters. Charles spent time with Lillian in the parlor: Lillian on the piano, Charles singing Schubert. Everyone thought Charles would marry Lillian, but she was as strong willed and feisty as he. It became apparent to both of them that they were not suitable for each other. He began a courtship of Alice. Though three years older, she was more demure and, in the end, accepted his proposal. Charles was ambitious. A Royalist by ancestry, he had landed in what had been staunchly Revolutionary territory, not far from Lexington and Concord. Perhaps driven by a need to prove himself, he eventually turned that dirt farm into a greenhouse operation and became the largest carnation grower in New England.

As he became successful and made money Charles took an interest in other things, including the stock market and race horses.

The smell of cigars followed Charles. The house smelled of cigars and his cars smelled of cigars. He loved big cars and always had four or five in the extended garage with a gas pump just outside the first bay. One of the cars was a Cadillac limousine, meant to be chauffeur driven. He used it as a truck, which he drove himself, with a load of carnation boxes in the back stacked on the velvet seats and jump seats. The Lincoln Zephyr was Alice's car. She drove around town even after she was blind as a bat. She knew the way to the library, the town hall and the Congregational Church and that was enough for her. Much of her time was spent at home.

After working in the greenhouse on Thursday mornings, Charles washed and dressed for driving the carnations to the flower market in Boston. He wore bespoke suits, white shirt and tie, spats and polished brown shoes. He buffed his nails till they shone. On his way home from Boston he stopped at Mrs. Elmira Lyons's, the widow who lived at the end of Clark Island Road, to help with small repairs, and afterward they would make music together. Mary Noyse, Alice's cousin who lived in the great Victorian place across the street would call Alice and let her know he was there.

Alice smiled vaguely, seemingly unaffected by her husband's flirtations and choleric moods. He was angry and disdainful, seemed bored with her. She never questioned or talked back.

Three

1981

Harriet was still living in the great Victorian pile where she and her sisters were born and raised. Her mother, Alice, was born in this house and had lived in it with her husband, given birth to four daughters and died in her bed on her eightieth birthday. Harriet, the third daughter, was the one in the house to take care of her parents in their old age. She was the daughter who did not marry, the one who became the librarian in town and stayed on. Loring Crankshaw offered to help Harriet Upchurch fix up the old house after the parents' death and later would help her move into the retirement community she had chosen for her final years. "Downsizing this large house to make it cozy and livable is not going to be easy," he told her. "I'd be happy to help you."

Crankshaw, a graduate of Harvard with a degree in architecture was handsome, witty and had good taste. Son of an artist, he knew how to set up a house, where to put the sofa, the rugs, the paintings, the side chairs and tables and what to leave behind. He'd known their family for years. He was a friend and they trusted him. They understood that he never seemed to have a steady job but would not accept any work that was beneath his idea of himself. Being a consultant for old people downsizing or moving into retirement villages was his idea of work that gave him class. He felt his charm and good taste was something they were lucky to get.

After six weeks and with Harriet's letter of recommendation, he apparently went on to a long string of frail and trusting widows, moving in with them while he got them settled. He knew how to charm them and escort them to concerts and dinner parties. He understood the subtleties of Boston and east coast culture and seemingly was born into it. He dressed well, supposedly helping himself to the Brooks Brothers' suits and shoes of dead husbands. He was well-spoken and an expert name dropper, familiar with names of old

Boston families, names he found in desks he cleared out. He spoke knowingly of Harvard professors, bankers and stock brokers, Boston Symphony instrumentalists, artists and writers. Old ladies were proud to be seen on the arm of this debonair young man and did not dismiss rumors of the possibility that he was a lover.

He felt his charm and good taste was something they were lucky to get. There were rumors about how he would help himself to some of the better pieces during a move. Small Chinese bowls, leather bound books, silver tea services; nothing anybody would notice right away, if ever.

He knew the Upchurch house well, had been with his father when he gave painting lessons to Alice and her friends *en plein air* or, on stormy days, still life or portraits inside. Foster had watched his father hang Alice's paintings on her dark walls as well as his own now famous paintings of New England barns. He admired the rugs, knew the story of how Alice collected these oriental rugs, rugs on top of rugs, a precious collection.

Harriet had not changed anything in the ten years she had lived with her parents in the house. The rugs upon rugs were on the floors, the toaster remained in the middle of the dining room table, the four poster beds were made up and ready for family or guests, the chess board sat on a bridge table in the parlor near the piano. When she wasn't working at the public library, Harriet played bridge with a group of old friends or rode her horse across the countryside. Once a year she went on a month long voyage, traveling by tramp steamers wherever they would take her around the world. Housekeeping was not her passion.

"The rocking chair will stay in your wing," Crankshaw announced.

"That old thing? It's worn and it's ugly."

"My dear Harriet, you have many fine qualities, but a sense of interior design is not one of them. The scruffy old rocking chair does not have beauty *per se*, but it has history. Your female ancestors rocked their babies in this chair. The men rocked away their arthritis and cares in old age. It's good to have one ugly piece in an elegant, tasteful room. It's a conversation piece."

"I don't give a damn about conversation pieces. It's a pathetic ruse for an uneducated person who doesn't have anything of interest to say."

"Trust me on this one, Harriet. You'll be happy we kept it."

When Harriet was settled in to her part of the house, the family weren't at all sorry to see the lovely rooms Crankshaw had created, furnished with the family furniture, the lesser pieces having been left in the other wing of the house for the auction to follow. Loring Crankshaw slept in this wing while he helped Harriet sort out and settle in. And when she was settled, he said, "A job is opening up for me in Virginia- if I could just stay on here with you a few more weeks – I'll try not to be a burden to you."

Four

2018

As they walked down the path to the beach through wildflowers and dappled sunlight Dorothy Tappertit said, "Isn't this beautiful?"

"Ticks," Loring Crankshaw grumbled.

"Are you always this negative?"

"Yeah I suppose you could say so. Women go for it. They like my grumpiness. When it's mixed with my suave and elegant side they find it sexy."

"At your age . . . or I should say at the age

of the women you're courting . . . I wouldn't think sexy would come into the equation."

"It does," Loring replied as he strolled on ahead.

Dorothy chattered on about one thing or another, as she tended to do as she aged—or so her grandchildren told her. "The beach is rocky, not a sand castle building venue. Our sand castles are in the air, dreams, hopes, houses we would want to live in. We build rock house buildings instead on this beach. The little boys always build forts. The little girls, houses, hotels and castles. Some rocks are huge boulders really. They are the basis of the buildings. The foundations. Smaller rocks are brought to the boulders from other parts of the beach to make ramparts, rooms, etc. I'm hoping it doesn't sound sexist to say the boys build forts and the girls, hotels but I can't help it. That's just what happens. This went on when our generation were children, when our children were children and our grandchildren too. We now have no one of the age to build. But on Sunday I was on the beach with a grand-niece. She was making people out of rocks. Lying down specimens put together on her boogie board. A four inch round rock for a head, a triangle for body. Sea weed for hair and what she called lasagna seaweed for clothes. These rock figures, forts and hotels, most of them, wash away in the tide." Dorothy barely noticed when Foster started back up the path.

"Hold on Loring. There's something I want to ask you. She grabbed his arm. I've heard that you might be just the person. My brother and sister-in-law live in Ontario. Priscilla has dementia and needs to go into one of those so-called retirement places. Parker decided rather than find one in Canada, it should be here in Plymouth near the family, hoping that he could spend most of his time in the Compound while she is incarcerated in Ocean View Acres or whatever the hell it's called."

Loring looked at this woman he hardly knew. He knew the type though. In fact one of them, Holly Nightbridge had asked him to stop in to see Dorothy. He had pretty much retired from his work, but this case had possibilities. He wouldn't have to act the suitor to some old bag. This one was apparently already half gone. The husband would be his client and he most likely wouldn't care. He wouldn't watch carefully. Loring knew him by reputation – Parker Tappertit was a former judge in Boston. There would be good antiques in the house, both American and Canadian.

"What's the proposal?" he asked. "Does your brother-in-law want to talk with me directly or through you? If we were to make a deal, I'd look over their condo in the Ocean View place here before flying up to Ontario. It would be best if they were there for a day or so with me before they leave in case I have questions or they have questions for me. Having looked over the place here I will have a sense of what they should bring here and what they should leave behind. Usually I make decisions based on peoples' desires, but often I have to be strict with my clients. Eventually they are happy with my suggestions. I gather from your earlier remarks that you have some question of my reliability. You've heard rumors of my accepting tips from some of the widows, or that I've ingratiated myself into their hearts. Am I to blame that they tend to fall in love with me, that they love having me as an escort?"

Dorothy phoned Parker the next day and told him that Loring Crankshaw had helped Ted's family years ago. He was remembered as being good at his work. Kind of a glorified decorator/consultant. Well worth having. She did not to go into his reputation. After all, none of the families he had helped were particularly bothered by the possibility that he was stealing things. The fact that he kept the old folks amused and happy during the stressful move, and even stayed on, outweighed his ill-gotten gains. He became a friend to those who were losing their friends to old age.

Dorothy was grinning with anticipation. She was not happy with her brother-in-law— stuffing Priscilla away into a nursing home so early in the game while romancing, and trying to move in with, her. She was looking forward to the drama about to ensue as Parker dealt with Crankshaw. These two old devils will meet their match.

Five

Loring Crankshaw was tired when he got into Toronto airport. His flight had been diverted to Montreal, and something held them there long enough to miss the connection to Toronto. He was three hours late getting in. He had told Parker Tappertit that he'd spend the night in Toronto and take a cab out to the cottage, all on Lloyd's bill, of course. He didn't tell him that. He knew that Tappertit wasn't the type to split hairs or be concerned about charges. Crankshaw had a few drinks at the hotel bar, grabbed a burger at a nearby McDonalds and went to bed. The next morning he took an Uber out to the Tappertit place, about forty miles north of Toronto. $150 Canadian. The car pulled up to an unpretentious house surrounded by English gardens, apple and peach orchards and a lavish blueberry field.

Parker Tappertit came out the door to greet him, hand held out. Beige corduroy pants, plaid shirt, tasseled loafers, baseball cap, handsome weathered face. Crankshaw knew the type. He was a typical Boston kind of guy, transplanted to Canada. But this was to be a different deal for Loring. Usually the husbands died first and the wives were left and needed help. The wives were glad of his masculine presence. They were wives who were used to acting subordinate. Wives who had not been touched by feminism. They were strong, smart females clever enough to allow their husbands to feel they were in charge, but still wanting a man around.

"My wife is inside," Parker said. "Just a word before we go in. She's gradually floating into dementia; she can't hold onto a thought for long. She has good days and bad days. You may not notice at first. She is able to put on a good face and it fools people. Later she gets angry at herself. It's the usual old age stuff I guess – You may have seen it before. One of our children—our daughter— will come up and fly with her tomorrow to Boston where she'll stay until the apartment is set up in the retirement place Plymouth. You've seen her place there, right? What I hope you'll do is chose the stuff to take, the stuff to leave and the stuff we should get rid of. We're hanging on to the house here. OK let's go in. I don't want her to think we're going behind her back, which of course we are," he chuckled.

What an ass, thought Loring. He must think I've never done this before. He said. "I understand. You have a nice place here. I'm looking forward to seeing inside." And a cup of coffee, he thought.

Priscilla was at the window, gazing out. Slender, white hair to her shoulders, with a tentative smile when she turned around to greet Loring.

"Hello, Mrs. Tappertit. I am impressed with your paintings. Your husband tells me you've studied in Oaxaca as well as Toronto and Paris.

"Thank you. But I haven't painted for some years, have I Parker?"

"Not as much lately, dear, but you'll get back to it. Sarah is arriving soon to fly with you tomorrow to Boston. I'll follow on Friday after we pack up a few things."

"Why?" Priscilla asked.

"We're moving to Plymouth."

"Oh no. Not for good."

"We'll see how it goes."

"Just the usual two weeks is all I can do. You know that."

"Let's talk about it when Sarah gets here."

Loring was wandering around the house making mental notes. His plan was to get into his work after Parker has left. Business had been poor lately. He saw a few small easily lifted things that wouldn't be missed.

"Priscilla, could you show Loring to the guest room. He'll be staying to do some work here."

"Oh how nice. Just come with me."

"The other direction to the stairs, dear."

Crankshaw took his suitcase and made small talk as he walked with Priscilla to the stairs, praising her paintings, asking about her fascinating life, surprised at how young she looked. She responded with girlish smiles. It didn't take him long to figure out the plan. Priscilla would be moving to a two bedroom apartment at Ocean View Acres in Plymouth. He had seen the place and knew the set-up. These assisted living places were pretty much the same. It would need a couch, two chairs, coffee table, lamp tables, dining table and four chairs in the living room; twin beds, bureau, bedside tables, rugs in the bedroom; desk, chair, pull out sofa, easy chairs and TV in the spare room. Some dishes, pots and pans, books. All easily chosen here without making a dent in the furnishings. They had obviously brought north more than they needed from Boston and scattered it around amidst the handsome well-chosen Canadian country pieces. Most of her paintings would go to Plymouth.

The daughter, Sarah, arrived in the late afternoon. She thinks she has met Loring Crankshaw but can't quite place him. She is suspicious both of him and of her father and his motives. "Mother doesn't seem that demented. What's the rush?"

"She has good days and bad. A call came in

this morning from one of my friends. He saw Priscilla out driving early yesterday morning.

'I was just running down to pick up the paper at the corner store,' she told me.

You're not following doctor's orders.' I said

'That bastard. I've always been a good driver.' She told me.

"I changed the subject and took away her car keys. I go with her to her therapist now as they have suggested. I go to all her doctors and other appointments, actually, so I can follow through and get hints of what's going on and what needs to be done. Far as I can figure out there is no medication or therapy that is working or will work. But they keep offering suggestions, making appointments with specialists, prescribing pills and getting paid. You'd think it would make Priscilla feel better—all this attention, all the hope—but through the fog and confusion a certain part of her brain works and you can see she's not taken in by the promises of the medicine men. I love the therapist Allison. Her method is a combination of Buddhism, Twelve Step acceptance, and Jewish wisdom. Not much in the way of Freud and Jung to confuse things. She calls herself a jew-bude. Apparently there are Unitarians called uni-budes and Episcopalians called episco-budes, etc. My Episcopalian friend who calls herself episco-bude; says she probably wouldn't "get it" if it weren't for Buddhist wisdom making sense of Christianity."

"C'mon Dad, get to the point."

"Well, Allison tells your mother to accept

her limitations and relax about her losses. She told me in an aside that if any shrink tells you he can cure your mental problems, leave and find a new one. I sit next to your mother on a couch facing Allison and take it all in for the three quarter hour visit. She's a beautiful woman – Allison. Of course your mother is too. I feel pretty happy sitting with these two lovely, clever and brilliant women, one out of it and one with it. Allison has only a few customers. I guess they're called clients, or patients. She is on the verge of retiring and considering moving down to the Cape Cod. So we've had some one on one conversations about life below the border. I've taken her out to supper a few times. Actually she seems a bit interested in me. She mentioned how I appear to understand her philosophy/

psychology. We both discovered Leonard Cohen late in life at about the same time and have that in common."

"Dad! Back to Mum and why you're moving."

"Your mother is too confused now to care or to understand. She makes herself focus on a few subjects of daily living. Breakfast, lunch and dinner, dressing, going to bed and getting up. She tries to answer the phone with the TV remote and tries to change the TV station with the telephone. She shuffles around with a worried look on her face. I remind myself of better times and try to ignore her irrational behavior. Her long term as well as short term memory is shot. Our love and joy together is in the moment: weather, birds, and phases of the moon. It's been a long angst filled year or two with stress and anger in the house. A year of many attempts to cure or at least cope with her mental problems, a year of many therapists, young kind men and women who start off feeling sure they can crack the code, get into the distorted thinking and come out the other side with solutions. It's been more than a year of figuring out how I fit into the scheme of such things. Years spent avoiding the problem, doing my own thing, staying away from distorted thinking but still loving. Now it's taken a new turn. She insists on marching to her own distant drummer. On top of her earlier anxiety, she now has dementia. She's losing her balance, losing her memory. She keeps her beauty, her bashful charm, her sense of humor, so that to the wide world she's fine; almost . . . until she takes a massive fall, or wanders away. The plan is that you and your mother will take off tomorrow."

Loring was quite taken by Priscilla. She was lovely, like a gentle fragile antique. They spent some time together alone in the guest-room where she floated about showing him the light switches and lamps, the way to the toilet, pointing out her paintings, how to pull the shades and draw the curtains. He couldn't understand why she was being put away. She had a great deal of sex appeal. Maybe it was romantic appeal. He was sorry that she would not be his client. He did not like Parker. But Parker would be the one he would be deal-ing with. He was going to suggest that Parker leave with his wife and daughter in the morn-ing. He already had the picture and plan. Just from their dinner table discussion and from his brief survey of the premises, he could make decisions on his own without being weighed down by the tiresome Parker. He talked with Priscilla as she showed him around his room. By asking such questions as how long they'd lived here, how did she spend her days, had she liked living in Boston, what family did she have, he was able to work out what she was like and what she would like to surround herself with in a new apartment in Plymouth. He was truly interested in her and she knew it. He could tell. And he, through sizing her up for the move, found she was interested in him. His father was an artist. She asked about him and his work trying to remember if she had seen his paintings. They sat on what was to be his bed and talked about art, about his family and hers. She reached over and took his hand. He knew she had dementia, but he also knew that this was not a demented act.

At 10 p.m. when the nurse who would help her to bed arrived, Parker called up the stairs to ask Priscilla and Loring to come down to say goodnight. Priscilla and her daughter would be leaving at noon the next day to catch the 3 p.m. flight from Toronto to Boston. The nurse went back upstairs with Priscilla. Loring joined Parker and Sarah at the table.

"Parker, I suggest you go along with your wife and daughter. I have a good sense of what to do here. I have already researched moving companies, checked on customs issues, taken measurements of your wife's new place in Plymouth. Your list of suggestions is good and complete. No need for you to stick around. I'm used to working alone."

Parker was reluctant. Sarah pushed him to do as Crankshaw suggested. She needed help with Priscilla. Crankshaw knew his business, had professional expertise.

So the three of them took off the next morning,

Crankshaw got to work with his list and put his colored sticky dots on furniture to indicate to the movers which pieces to move (red), stay (blue), or toss (yellow).

Six

Plymouth

Ted can't stop thinking about the rug. How did it get out of the family's hands? How many other things were stolen? Certainly someone in the family must have wanted that rug or should at least have held on to it. There were so many memories attached. Or was that only true for him? Was it because his life had been lived in other countries that he hung on to childhood memories most fiercely. He has one brother who has four children. There were three cousins including Nancy. Why didn't someone watch over the family treasures more carefully? He couldn't stop wondering. But he really wanted to get on with other interests now that he was retired and had time.

Sue fit into Plymouth life nicely. She was on the Historical Society Board of Directors, played tennis and was involved in conservation activities. They were both helping with plans for the great 400th anniversary of the arrival of the Mayflower. He had a lot of ideas he'd like to float. But thoughts of the rug kept cropping up. Could it be, as his cousin Nancy had inferred, that Crankshaw just simply rolled it up and took it off to some storage barn and later sold it and nobody noticed? The guy reeked of that kind of thing. Mainly because he looks like one of us and nobody would suspect he was a bounder.

I can't decide whether to pursue this line of thinking or not, Ted thought. Where would I do research, where would I go to try to research the rug's provenance? The Snodgrasses are set with the rug. They wouldn't want their life upset by the questions that would need to be asked. And besides this, I'm just not feeling well. Don't know what it is but I would rather not add stress and uncertainty to my life at this point.

"Sue," he called to his wife in the kitchen. "I think I'd better go for a check-up. I'm not feeling well."

"Shape up, Ted. You're spending too much time obsessing about that damn rug. Go take a walk around the pond."

"Thanks for the sympathy. I'm going to make an appointment to see Dr. Berry tomorrow."

"You did really well," the boy-faced doctor beamed at him as if he'd scored the winning goal. "The colonoscopy went well. No polyps, just a bit of swelling." The presiding nurse was less congratulatory. "We must get rid of the air before you go."

"Do you mean out the rear?" Sue, sitting at Ted's bedside, asked. The man with the gray beard in the next bed was burping and farting and not even awake yet. Ted, well known by his boyhood friends for his talent of farting on demand—not quite up to the National Anthem but impressive anyway—did not make a peep in the post-op room in endoscopy. He might have been at a debutant ball.

Boy doctor said, "I'll send a complete report," as he turned to leave.

"Wait a minute!" called Sue. "The whole point of our visit to your office and of having this operation was our primary care physician's order that we see you to try to figure out what's wrong with Ted's life. You aren't supposed to brush him off with a multi thousand dollar colonoscopy which, judging from the crowd here this Tuesday in the middle of May, is the place to be. The place to see and be seen. What we are looking for is suggestions for a change of diet or more exercise to cure whatever ails him. Not these tiresome and expensive tests. I want hands on care here. Recommendations of less sugar, keep your hands out of the cookie jar, and do more crossword puzzles. That's what the doctors on late night TV say is the trick, as the camera pans to smiling nodding sycophants in the audience."

The next week, with no interesting results from the colonoscopy, Sue sat in a small waiting room, while Ted was in a neurologist's office. She told Ted that after today's round of doctor appointments, she was bowing out of his search for the Holy Grail: for a magic pill that would cure whatever was bothering him. He had either quit or been rejected, one could say ejected, from programs and experiments from here to Washington by way of Boston. She's sitting in her third Muzak infused doctor's office waiting room of the day, as Ted moves in a fog from one MD to another searching for a cure for the incurable, a cure for the person he is who is caught in a maze of minor mental and physical disorders. He keeps searching for a solution for what makes him restless, short-tempered, angry, rude, selfish, etc. In the first two waiting rooms the flat screen TV blared out music as a background to advertisements for pills, showing a stroke victim describing his miraculous cure; then diabetes victims, then Alzheimer's, described by a trendy baby-voiced beauty with big smile, big hair, big breasts. All the while a crawl goes along the bottom of the screen letting the watchers know that the pope has asked priests to offer forgiveness to women who have had abortions; word of a train crash in New Delhi killing 125; Trump disputing the necessity for face masks, all in counterpoint to the muzak, scroll, and magic pills. After Ted is dismissed by the neurologist they go on to the next muzak-filled waiting room for blood-letting per instructions from the primary care doctor (of the first waiting room fame: who kept them waiting one hour). The blood-letting was ordered so that Ted could be part of a nationwide study on Alzheimer's (the Alzheimer's Association had scads of funds, donated by rich guilt infused widows, searching for ways to spend it.) The blood-letting was quick. Just one or two repeats of the TV scroll. The urine giving did not take long either.

Sue and Ted had studied languages when they were posted overseas to embassies. Now they were trying to learn the language of medicine, terms such as: MRI, hippo campus, pancreas, chronic changes, psa level, cat scan. However, it became clear that part of

Ted's problem was his anxiety and outrage about the rug and Crankshaw.

Sue suggested he get away for a while. Their small cabin in New Hampshire needed to be checked. They hadn't been there for years. He could get away there, be on his own, and relax.

Ted got to the cabin at about five pm. The key was behind the shutter. He pulled it out and fit it in the lock. The place was dank and unwelcoming but he was glad of that. He needed to get away and forget the last two months. He opened the windows, lit a fire in the log burning stove, looked out to the mountains and started to feel relaxed. He went back to the car, took out the cooler and his duffle bag, and brought them into the cabin. Mice were scratching along the floor, flies began to wake as the cabin warmed and buzz on window sills.

"Hello everyone. You are to be my best friends for the week. I'm letting you all stay, have your way, do what you want. No fly swatters, no mouse poison or traps."

He flopped in the birch log chair, its green cushion mildewed, and looked out the window toward Mt. Lafayette. He noticed a crow sitting on a stump down the hill. "Wait. What the hell?" he said aloud to his pals the mice and flies. "When did that pine tree get cut and who gave permission?" He felt himself beginning to get enraged. Then told himself not to think about it. He was here to get away and relax. But it was outrageous that someone came on the property even though it is posted. He sat down and worked

on the relaxation and meditation exercises
he'd been taught.

A loud gunshot sounded. He stood up and
looked out. The crow on the stump was now
dead on the ground. Damn. Shooting here is
not supposed to happen. He went outside. A
disreputable middle-aged man was swagger-
ing toward him, 22 on his shoulder.

"Hello, old man. I saw your car and got rid
of the crow for you."

"Wait. Who are you? How dare you hunt
on this property? Can't you read the sign?"

"I've been looking after the property for
you. Just call me the Good Samaritan. Bad
luck to have a crow on a stump don't you
know. I cut that tree for you last week. It
gives you a better view across the valley to the
mountains."

"I never wanted that tree cut. What are you up to?"

"I'm taking care of the place, as I told you."

"But it doesn't need taking care of."

"Oh yeah? I cleaned the gutters, patched the roof, and replaced a broken window."

"Get out. Go away. I want to be alone."

"Why? You're not as young as you used to be. You need help. And I'm happy to give it to you no charge. Nobody's been here for years. The place was falling apart. OK. I'll leave while you settle in, but I'll be back tomorrow. Before I go I'll hang the crow by its leg on your clothesline. That'll scare away the other crows and will bring good luck, peace and harmony to you. I'll bring you coffee tomorrow morning."

Ted woke up in a hospital bed with Jack

sitting next to him. "Jack!? What the hell is going on? Where am I? What are you doing here?"

"Take it easy, Pop. You were in an accident. I'm not sure what happened, but you're here in the Portsmouth, New Hampshire hospital. I got the call because they found my address on some papers you had on you. I called Mum. She said you were staying at the cabin for the week. I gather you were on your way home. You got off pretty easy. Just a broken leg, a concussion and some scratches."

"Oh for God's sake. When I got to the cabin there was some weird nosey neighbor who kept hanging around trying to be, as he said, a Good Samaritan. I stayed a couple of days and took off. All I wanted to do was to be alone and sort myself out. Did I hit another car? Was anybody else hurt? What's the state of my car?"

"I don't know anything. Just got here myself."

"It's good to see you Jack. Been a long time. Is this what I have to do to get you to visit? Just kidding. Can you stay a while? Tell me how things are. You still going out with that gorgeous Irish girl? Did I ever tell you about when my father ended up in the hospital in Florida?"

"No. I thought Grandpa never went to doctors or hospitals. He always said that's the way you get sick."

"Well, here's the story. I got the call from their private nurse on Saturday night. She was beside herself with apologies, explaining that because she had not instructed her

overnight replacement in detail your grandpa
who had fallen out of bed, had been trucked
off in an ambulance to the Del Ray Hospital.
I caught the next flight out of Boston and
took a cab from West Palm airport directly
to the hospital. He was in the intensive care
place plugged into tubes bringing stuff into
his body and taking stuff out. He was coma-
tose. I told the head nurse to unplug him. She
said she couldn't without the doctor's orders
and the doctor would not be in until noon on
Monday.

"I went to the apartment to be with your
Grandma.

'Where's Harry?' she asked.

"I called my brother and sister to tell them
that he seemed to be on his way out. Frank
couldn't get away (we both knew that Pop

wouldn't want him to see him that way.) Julie flew in from Los Angeles.

"The three of us, Grandma, Julie and I, went to the hospital at noon on Monday. The old man was lying in state, looking rather well with all the nutrients and oxygen pumping him up, filling in his wrinkles. The head nurse came in to chat. She told us she was from Maine. One of Maine's finest, grandpa would have said: a tall buxom blond of a certain age with life experiences written on her face.

"She told us that after Grandpa was brought in and hooked up, he sat up in his bed and yelled, 'I'm getting out of here.'

"She said she took his hand and said, 'Take me with you!'

"This may have accounted for the happy

peaceful look on his face. Grandpa, as you may remember, was a flirt. He liked smart and beautiful girls (like Grandma) and was of the opinion that one of these traits did not over-rule the other.

"A large terrifying man came into the room. His long white hair was pulled into a pony tail. He had gross heavy features, thick lips, large nose, coke bottle glasses in front of his bloodshot eyes. He spoke loudly in a New York accent. 'He's going down for an EKG in ten minutes. I ordered a brain scan and X-rays. Some blood work.'

"'Wait a minute,' I said. 'Are you the doctor?'

'Yeah. I am.'

'Well, we are his family and we do not want, and he doesn't need, those tests.'

'We want to see what´s going on,' he yelled.

'No we don't,' I yelled back. 'We know what's going on. He's dying and we want you to un-attach him.'

He stood fuming, his face getting redder. 'I´ll let the nurse know.'

Grandma said, 'What´s taking so long?'

'At least he can keep track of the stock market,' Grandma said pointing to the heart monitor graph on the wall.

'Why is the oxygen still attached? Julie asked.

'To help him breathe,' said the nurse.

'But you're not supposed to breathe when you're dying. Please remove it.'

'What's taking so long?' asked Grandma again. 'They shoot horses.'

Afterward we went back to the apartment complex (lovingly called retirement community). An old codger pushed his walker toward us as we got out of the car. 'How is Harry?' he asked.

'He's dead.'

'What did he die of?'

'Old age.'

'How old was he?'

'Eighty-five'

'That´s nothing. I´m ninety-two.'

'It was old enough for Harry,' your grandmother said.

"He had stopped eating two weeks earlier to hasten his demise because he had no intention of hanging around with old folks shuffling around with walkers. He made that quite clear. As it was, he had lived longer than anyone in his family, a testament to your grandmother's good cooking and his athletic life. He smoked two packs of Camels a day, always had one dangling from his mouth on the tennis court, working at the farm, or skiing.

I drove his car to the recommended undertaker's office to make 'arrangements.'

"Cremation," I told the sharkskin suited man who met me.

"He opened folding doors to reveal a wall length cabinet displaying the urn collection. Urns with golf players on the top, sailboats, motorboats, Fido, grandchildren, hearts and flowers.

"'You can honor Dad with one to fit his hobby or interest,' he oozed.

"Dad?!! Who are we talking about? We never called him Dad, I was outraged. As you know, we called him by his first name, the old man, or Pop.

"I told him that a cardboard box would do that we were taking him to the family cemetery in Massachusetts.

"Ah. And what cemetery is that.

"I told him. He said he would have to check. Some cemeteries require that the cremains be placed in a cement or steel box.

Cremains?! I asked, 'Why is that.'

'In case it becomes necessary to move Dad.'

"Why are you telling me this," Jack asked.

"Just want you to know what you will face when I kick the bucket."

"C'mon Pop. Gimme a break. You're not going to die. You're too mean to die."

"Yeah?! Just wait and see"

Seven

P arker drove to the Compound and dropped in at the Guest House to say hello to Dorothy before the pot luck dinner at the Big House. Dorothy was delighted to see him. She was ready for her evening restorative rum and did not like to drink alone. "I read somewhere," she said, "that it behooves lonely women to take on the burden of the world's drinking."

"Well, I'd be happy to join you. Rum and tonic is fine for me. Include lonely men in the piece." They settled comfortably on the porch with their drinks plus crackers and cheese.

"My grandson has been using me and my frustrations in his routine at the Comedy Club in Cambridge," Dorothy said. "His rendition of an old lady trying to remove the paper from a bouillon cube seems to have set them howling in Central Square. Of course yelling at the TV; throwing the cell phone across the room, etc. apparently had built the audience up to their frenzy of laughter. Grumpy old folks apparently make good copy." Dorothy and Parker chatted comfortably about one thing and another and finally moved across to join the younger generations who had gathered in the Big House for a pot luck supper. Ted and Sue had been invited and walked in with and Paul and Dorothy. Sue carried a large pot of ratatouille. He was on crutches and immediately began to agitate about Crankshaw and the issue of his family's rug.

A storm was coming as they ate dinner. The sky turned black pushing away fat fluffy clouds and blue sky. They sat around after dinner playing monopoly or chatting. It was hot and humid, beginning to rain. Nobody wanted to get up to close windows or put down outside umbrellas shading the tables. They felt safe. Parker's grandmother, who was desperately afraid of lightning, had installed lightning rods on the house. This gave them a false sense of security. 'Them' didn't include Dorothy. She had recently weeded a bed on the northwest side of the house. She saw that the lighting rod wasn't grounded. She had meant to do something about it but didn't know whom to call. It was more than a hundred years ago when the thing was put in. She was hot and tired. Muggy heavy heat preceded the lightning they could see moving toward them across the ocean. The dog was a mess. Every time thunder clapped she pounced on another lap. Dorothy bought Broadway to add to Park Place, and then sat back and looked around the room.

Each summer this house fills with family and friends (though some years when the trim needs painting or new plumbing is required they rent it for a week or two to bring in some income.) Smells and memories cling to the furniture. Cigarette burns remain on the edges of tables, gin rings are scattered on top. Cats have sharpened their nails and shredded corners of the couch slipcover. The dress-up boxes at the end of the guest room closet exude moths. Rejected wedding presents through the ages are arranged in the corner cupboard of the dining room. Demitasse cups, the once shining silver bowls (they wonder every year whose initials are those etched on the side.) Five generations have left their mark. Names or initials and dates are written beside the lines drawn on a corner post to measure heights of children through the years. Some of those boys and girls shot up between the ages of nine and fifteen; some stayed dormant until age fifteen and then overtook the steady growers. Dog piddles have left stains on rugs. When extreme high tides hit during the nor'easter last March the banking eroded and the Guest House began to slip over the cliff edge, there was talk of letting the small Guest House go, tearing down this so-called Big House and building in their places one sensible year-round house. The family just couldn't make that decision.

The thunder came ten seconds after the lightning.

The storm was coming closer.

Sally bought the fourth railroad. Fred landed on Chance and went directly to Jail, did not pass Go, did not collect $200. Sue put two hotels on the greens. Dorothy's turn. She was handing the money over to buy a house on Broadway when the lightening hit a metal chair on the porch, leapt over to the drainpipe travelled up and crashed through an upstairs window. No damage done but it was nervous making

Afterward Ted and Sue joined Dorothy and Parker for coffee and brandy on the deck of the Guest House to watch the sunset. The thunderstorm had moved on. They chatted about Parker's recent move to Plymouth from Ontario. "I don't mind giving things away or donating to charity but I don't like the idea of people going behind my back – stealing. A friend of mine's mother in a Florida senior living place was bilked of over a thousand dollars by her home health care person who was forging her name on checks she was writing to herself. Nobody noticed for years. I'm worried about this character Crankshaw. How do I know whether he's taken stuff? Certainly he has had the opportunity. I left him alone in the house. He decided what to pack and send off. I will have no idea if he took stuff until I finally miss it. Like Ted, finding that rug forty years later."

"I prefer to have someone take what he

wants," said Dorothy. "I need to get rid of stuff and have a hard time deciding what should go. Everything seems to bring up a fond memory attached to it. If it were stolen I wouldn't feel the loss. If I give it away or sell it I'll feel responsible for breaking a link. For getting rid of something with meaning."

'That's nuts."

"Maybe I'm a socialist or communist. Also I feel the weight of having to care for things."

"Then you support Loring Crankshaw and his methods?" Ted asked.

"Sure. What's wrong with what he does? He gives new life to sad lonely widows. He builds them up, admires them, points out their good character traits, their beauty. Also, he gets rid of stuff that bogs them down, ugly things that have been in the family too long.

He sets up their living space with elegance and tastefulness. He even throws out old unattractive clothes I hear. Tell me, how is Priscilla doing? I purposefully haven't been to call yet. Loring Crankshaw told me that in general the advice given at Ocean View is to let the residents settle into their new life without bringing on old baggage. Not even family. Seems a bit rough, but they are successful. They know what they are doing."

"I don't like being called old baggage," Parker said. "Though I'm relieved not to be her keeper. But I'm sure she wants to see me. She's depended on me for years. I gather Crankshaw is keeping an eye on her and knows what he's doing. He suggested he stay on in her spare room to see her through the settling in period. I'm curious about stories of

J H BARTLETT

his taking things but I guess as you say what is it but stuff and maybe he deserves it. Don't you find it's odd that he's living there with her?"

"That seems to be his way."

"What have you discovered about the rug, Ted?"

Sue answered for him, "Ted became sick about it and has had a long series of tests to see if there is a physical component to his anxiety and depression. He felt he was being taken advantage of. He and his family. That rug seems to have had some mystical control over him. He tried to relax at the cabin in New Hampshire, but some well-meaning busy body kept dropping by to "help" him. That's when he drove home in a fury and had the accident. I think he's trying to let it go and has signed up for yoga and mindfulness classes. I can't imagine him actually going through with it."

"Give it a rest Sue," Ted grumbled.

Eight

"Could you stop over after lunch? We have something to ask you." Ted asked his daughter, Diane, on the phone.

"OK. What time? I have to finish a paper I'm writing.

"Three o'clock would be fine."

Diane wasn't happy about this. She was pretty sure she knew what they wanted, but when her father asked, she obeyed.

"Thanks for coming," he said. "We think you're the one to do this. You live closest. You have the law degree."

"So I know what it is. You want me to sign your living will. I told you I don't want to be the one to decide whether the time is right or not."

"It's all written right here. No extraordinary means."

"You may think that's simple and well defined. But it's not. You've got to get your doctor or lawyer or whomever wrote the damned thing to be specific. I can't believe they could expect anyone to sign this. I'm not going to pull the tubes out unless I see in writing exactly what you expect."

"Oh for god's sake. Everyone's doing it. Everyone we know has a living will. You'll know when the time comes what to do."

"Not true. Jack and I never agree on anything. Don't make me the one. He'll accuse me of killing you off too early or not soon enough."

After she left, Sue said, "I told you we should have asked Jack. Diane is so literal. She has to dot every I and cross every T."

"Jesus. You're right. We should have asked Jack or one of the cousins. They never would have even questioned the form. All it needs is a signature."

Meanwhile Ted was getting more involved in Plymouth "issues" especially plans for the 400th celebration of the landing of the Pilgrims. He loved the town and was touched by the warm welcome he'd been given. Sue's family had been summer people for generations but not involved in town politics. Their

Plymouth time was spent at the pond, reading, sailing, swimming, partying, singing, dancing. The only trips away from the area of their cottage were for food shopping and trips to the dump. For years in the past going to the Plymouth dump on Saturdays was a social occasion in itself.

Ted was fascinated as he got to know Plymouth people at how different they were, these Pilgrim progeny, from those he grew up with, whose ancestors including his own were Puritans. The Pilgrim story was that of breaking off from the Church of England. The Puritans who arrived in America a few years later set off to purify the church. Their nature was a culmination of 19th century patrician, Calvinist hard work and aspirations, comingled with a concerted effort to transcend the vestiges of elitism and privilege. Maybe a subtle difference, but noteworthy nonetheless and perhaps worth paying attention to for the 400th anniversary.

In his travels as a diplomat around the world, he did not find much interest in the fact that Plymouth happened to be where the Mayflower brought the first settlers. What people worldwide were fascinated by in those days was the melting pot, the great successes and inventiveness that happened on American soil. None of it perfect but better than in most of the rest of the world. Ted thought of the recent Plymouth Town Meeting. That would be something the rest of the world would like to see. Plymouth is an amalgam of historic houses, tattoo parlors, museums, Mexican, Italian, Thai, and seafood restaurants, a replica of the Mayflower, tee shirts, the Rock, windmills, nuclear power plant, cranberries, rope making factory, condos. Pilgrims were more fun loving than Puritans: in early days they wore colorful clothes vs. the Puritan black and white, they were welcoming, and still are joyful, open to immigrants, visitors, new ideas. There was a tradition of getting along. Thanks perhaps to the Mayflower Compact.

Ted was able to research his grandmother's rug journey from her house to the Snodgrass house in Plymouth. He found along the way details of its provenance that need not be made public involving the selling of the rug by an historical society to get money to repair the roof. This was before the era when such things were closely watched, when one had to be careful to keep records and be transparent, when donations are made to charitable organizations and tax write offs are involved. Ted realized he did not want to open that whole can of worms. He was happy the rug was nearby. He was happy for the memories it brought up. He was trying to get over his hatred of Loring Crankshaw but not trying too hard. Such a shoddy character. Moving in with the lovely Priscilla Tappertit, who was only half alive. Taking advantage. But then apparently it's not true. Dorothy tells him Priscilla is enjoying a new life with Loring while Dorothy, herself, is shacking up with her brother-in-law, Parker, who had been apparently pursuing her for some time. These old age romances were unappetizing to Ted. He decided to check with others who had hired Loring Crankshaw so he could put together information for people who were considering hiring him. He would like to give a warning and put a halt to the scoundrel's illicit activities.

Ted called Holly Nightbridge. Her mother had engaged Crankshaw when she moved from her large house in Lexington to Fox Hollow, an assisted living place in nearby Sudbury. Holly invited Ted to lunch and afterward to visit the facility. She was under the impression that he wanted to move and was looking around for a retirement community.

"What I want to ask you is how the move went. Was your family happy with the services of Loring Crankshaw? Were you?'

"Why do you ask? I would think that with all the moves you've made in the Foreign

Service, this would be a piece of cake. Sue must have overseen dozens of moves."

Holly was sitting at her polished mahogany dining room table. The silver tea service on the sideboard behind her was reflected in the gold leaf framed mirror hanging on the wall. Holly herself was well preserved wearing a lime green golf shirt and plaid Bermuda shorts. An old Labrador sat at her feet adjusting slowly his position when she moved hers to make a point

"I'm not planning a move myself but am wondering whether to recommend Crankshaw to some cousins in Canada who need help with their move back to Plymouth into an assisted living place."

"Oh yes. Now I remember. You are Dorothy's cousin or is it brother in-law. I believe Loring stopped in to see her some months ago."

"You're right. The truth is Crankshaw has already been employed by the family. There are a few questions I have about him though. Was there anything out of the ordinary or perhaps unethical about his work for your family?"

"No. On the contrary. We were delighted. Mother loved him. He really cared about her. They became close friends. He was part of the family during the moving period. He had Thanksgiving with us. He moved in with her while she got settled at Fox Hollow, oversaw the arrangement of the furniture, the hanging of the pictures. He seemed to have a good sense of what to take to the new place and what to keep or throw out."

"Did you notice anything missing after the move? Were his charges fair and what you expected?"

"I don't think anything was missing. I didn't have an inventory of before and after. I could check with my sister. Though I must admit we're not a careful family about such things. What's a few pieces of silver or a crystal bowl in the great scheme of things? Overall we were happy. The transition was easy for mother and I think it was largely due to Loring Crankshaw."

"Do you know anyone else who hired Crankshaw?"

After he left and with Holly Nightbridges recommendation, Ted called David Childs from his cell phone in the car and stopped at his office in Boston an hour later.

"Oh yes, I knew he was lifting a thing or two. Nothing anyone cared much about. For all I knew my mother was giving him stuff as presents. Good riddance I say. Her place was a rat's nest of stuff. Good stuff and useless stuff all in together. I didn't envy him the job. She had stacks of magazines. Twenty years of National Geographics at least. And Audubon Society monthly reports. Letters, postcards, handmade presents from the grandchildren. She never threw out a snapshot. We all offered to help but she refused. Crankshaw knew how to persuade. He must have carried hundreds of boxes to the dump. Sure he was stealing from her. More power to the poor bastard. His was a thankless job from my point of view. Mother was in a state after Dad died. She was wandering around the house talking to herself most days. We hadn't realized how much she depended on him. She was too proud to let any of us help. Someone told us about Loring Crankshaw. I was impressed when he came to meet us at Mother's.

He sat right down and began talking with her about butterflies. How he knew about this passion of hers I have no idea. Crankshaw was well dressed and well spoken. She may have thought he was one of the family, one of the children she wished she had rather than the ones she did have. Anyway from that first interview on she was like putty in his hands. He praised her beauty, her youthfulness, her lovely house and its contents. Her move went smoothly and whatever it cost in lost family treasure was well worth it."

Eliot Overshoe agreed with Ted. "The guy was a scam artist. He was stealing things left and right. Two Persian rugs, a small British writing desk, Duncan Phyfe chairs, my father's leather saddle. We got insurance on some of the stuff but not enough. I couldn't stand the SOB. All airs and graces, pretending he is from some old family, dropping names of people, and of clubs. Claimed he went to Harvard. If you can put the finger on him, Ted, and get the police involved it would be a great service to all the elderly—the senior citizens as we're called—who potentially will be ripped off by bastards like him. There ought to be some registration of these people, a license, to show before the so-called consultant/decorator bastard moves in and steals family treasures from old defenseless family members."

Nine

While he waited for the moving van to arrive in Plymouth from Ontario, Loring Crankshaw stayed at a senior living place nearby in Duxbury in the apartment of an earlier client. A gentle lovely old girl who was delighted that he had chosen her to be the one to stay with. He helped her hang a few portraits they hadn't gotten to earlier and told her he would love to take her to an opening exhibit at the Museum of Fine Arts

Ted's cousin, Nancy, saw them sitting at a

table when she walked into the restaurant in downtown Plymouth where she was to meet Ted. She was quite sure it was Loring Crankshaw. Did Ted notice him, she wondered. Crankshaw had aged since he had bilked their family. Nancy didn't want to be in the middle of whatever might ensue if Ted knew he was here. Loring of course was with an old woman. Obviously he was still at his game. Looking handsome and debonair in a double breasted navy blazer, rep tie, tasseled loafers, fawning all over the old girl, oozing charm. Nancy wondered how far along they were in the relationship. The old lady looked slightly confused and dazzled at the same time. Her pearls in place, a double strand, a well fitted little blue suit, almost matching her blue hair. Had he performed his service already for his lunch companion or was he leading up to it, assuring her he wouldn't charge much, just a small amount to make her comfortable. It was a business arrangement but a special one just for her. He had a well-paying job at a small bank in Rhode Island, he told her, and didn't need the money. It's just that he enjoyed her company.

Ted and Nancy had lunch and chatted about family. He did not see Crankshaw. "There's something I haven't mentioned yet," Nancy told Ted. "Aunt Harriet told me, on her deathbed actually, that she had always lived with shame and guilt. She was sent away to New York at the age of seventeen supposedly to study cooking. She hadn't wanted to go to college as her sisters had done. She didn't even want to go off to boarding school. She wasn't a good student. She wasn't good at sports.

"She had fallen in love with one of the guys who worked in the greenhouse. They used to meet in the boiler house and kiss. It led on from that. She got pregnant. Grandma was shocked. They didn't say anything to anyone. Those were the days when one didn't talk about such things, especially in Puritan Massachusetts. Grandma found a place for her, an orphanage outside of New York City. She could have the baby there and give it up for adoption. But it turned out after the birth, as often happens, Harriet wanted to keep the baby and stay with him. Eventually she was turned out of the orphanage and taken in by one of Grandma's cousins who lived in Rochester. Harriet stayed with her for a few months. The baby, a boy, was given up for adoption. Harriet tried to find who and where but to no avail. She enrolled in a res- taurant school for a year, moved back to Boston and lived alone in a small apartment on Marlborough Street. She got a job in a restaurant and moved up the ladder to head cook/nutritionist in charge. She was a bitter and angry woman for many years. Eventually she made amends with her parents and would spend every other weekend in the fam- ily house in East Middleton. By the time she was forty she was ready to leave Boston and move home for good. She became the pub- lic librarian in Middleton. It worked well. As the parents aged she was there for them in the house where they could live out their lives without moving to a nursing home. Aunt

Harriet took to the bottle for a while, but gave it up in her sixties. I believe she made one or two attempts to track down her son, but without luck. She was never a warm loving person, but she got through life. She considered moving to a smaller place after Grandma and Grandpa died. She asked Loring Crankshaw for advice. He was about mid twenty at the time, just out of Harvard graduate school and about to go into a decorating business in Boston. He said he'd be happy to help but suggested first they look into her remaining in a wing of the house and rent out the rest to help pay expenses. She agreed – she really didn't care much about where she lived. She told him to work out a plan and she'd look it over. As he was working on the plans, he apparently started putting the moves on her.

I was wide-eyed as she told me this. She was pushing forty. She told me she'd never had a relationship after the baby. She felt old and dried up. Loring Crankshaw apparently made himself quite irresistible. She was reluctant at first. He told her he'd never known anyone as beautiful. He loved her looks, her gentle proud spirit, her intelligence. He told her he was drawn to her, he loved her. He found it so exciting to be with her. Meanwhile he was working up a plan for her to age in place as they put it now. She told me she was amazed to believe how attracted he was to her. Slowly through the months the attraction became mutual.

"Loring Crankshaw collected and placed some of the furniture and valuables into the east part of the house and placed the rest in the west side to be offered to the family. Now we come to the question of the rug you asked about, Ted. As I remember the things to go to auction were offered to the family first. No one in the family had a place for it. Crankshaw placed it for some time in the east side of the house for Harriet. It didn't fit in the small living room she made for herself so he rolled it up and told her he'd hang on to it for a while in case she changed her mind. By this time he had moved in with her, living there as he continued to redecorate the house and dispose of the unwanted stuff. The family didn't know they had formed a romantic relationship or that he had moved in but were happy to see how beautifully he had arranged things and how happy Harriet seemed. He told her that he planned to stay on while she got settled, and that a job was waiting for him in a bank in Virginia.

"After about a month he moved out. Aunt Harriet said she was devastated. He had told her he would love her forever. It was sudden and he never called. Some years later, when she was ready to move on to assisted living, she called him for help with the move. By then he had a number of customers. He had become the person to go to for help, for old people downsizing at various stages. He agreed to help Harriet and the romance blossomed once again. He had another auction of the stuff that he felt should not go on to her small apartment. He helped her sell the old family house and he moved in with her at the assisted living place for a while telling her he had never stopped loving her, never wanted to leave her, but felt it best for both if they didn't see each other or communicate as it was all they could do in their particular situation. He asked if he could move in with her telling the family it was just until his job in Rhode Island opened up. Crankshaw is a man who enjoys the conquest. Once he had dropped his "love bomb," as my neighbor calls it, and gotten his target to love him in return, he was satisfied. You may find this has been his *modus operandi* through the years. However, I don't believe that his targets—the women he ravished—will want to talk about it. It's a bit embarrassing and borders on shameful for some females to admit they've been taken in."

"That's quite a story, Nancy." Ted said. "It explains a lot, but it doesn't make things any better. This has got to stop. I feel badly for Parker Tappertit. Crankshaw performed his services for his wife and is indeed now living with her right here in Plymouth."

When the moving truck arrived from Ontario, Crankshaw met it at Ocean View Acres and instructed the moving men where to place the furniture and boxes. Two days later he called Parker and told him the place was all set up. He made the recommendation that Parker drop off Priscilla but not to stay with his wife while she got settled. It's better to make it clear from the beginning that this would not be a place for both of them. Actually, Parker did not plan to move in and was happy for this advice. Happy and relieved.

Priscilla was glad to see Crankshaw.

The apartment looked like home – already lived in. Crankshaw had bought flowers that he had arranged in a vase for the table and plants for the south facing windows. Twin beds were set up in her bedroom and a pull-out couch in the spare room decorated as a library. Her clothes were hung in her closet and folded into bureau drawers. Sheets and towels in the linen closet. A small amount of kitchen ware—pots, pans and other equipment—was stored in cabinets in the small kitchen. Table settings for four. She felt quite at home.

"I will be staying on for a few days to get you settled," Crankshaw told her. "I'll help hang the pictures, buy things you might find lacking and make sure you're comfortable. Parker is staying in the family compound right down the road. He'll visit now and then but won't actually live here."

Though there was a good restaurant on the first floor of Ocean View Acres, Loring and Priscilla ate in most evenings. They liked being alone with each other. Priscilla was a good cook, Loring did the shopping.

"I hope it's all right if I stay in the spare room for a while. I have a job coming up in Connecticut later in the month, and I want to be sure you are settled. I enjoy very much being with you, but I don't want to take advantage of you."

"I'd love to have you stay. I have not felt so calm and happy in years." Priscilla had never fit in with the Tappertit family. Summers in the compound, which everyone else in the family adored, were pure hell for her. Her mother-in-law was mean and she found her nastiness hard to take, though others in the family laughed it off. She didn't think of Ocean View as part of Plymouth. Her earlier Plymouth angst was nonexistent in this new place. She really hoped that the family would leave her alone. Maybe later she would like to see her children and grandchildren, but not until she was more settled.

Ten

"There's nothing wrong with you according to all the tests," Sue said to Ted. "Your problem is that you're furious about the rug and about all the junk your family lost because you weren't around to keep an eye on things.

Sue and Ted were sitting on Adirondack chairs watching a race in the pond – small cat boats around the buoy. Ted loved these boat races but he can't hold on to the joy and fun today. "I'm outraged that asshole has moved in with Priscilla flaunting his nastiness in my face right down the road. He is a crook and everyone knows it."

"There's no proof of that, Ted. Some people claim he has a reputation for lifting a few things, but most people don't really care. They are relieved to be rid of stuff. Think it through, Ted. What a burden it would be if you had held on to all your family's stuff, not just rugs but furniture, china, silver, crystal, table cloths. All that stuff is a burden these days."

"Not so. It is our family legacy. Our children and theirs are much the poorer for not having things to remind them of the ancestors. I haven't told you that I'm quite a way through my research on the provenance of our family rug here in town. It was put up for auction after it left my grandmother's house.

Apparently there was no room for it in Aunt Harriet's apartment when she moved out of the family house. So Crankshaw put it up for auction and the rug was bought by the Glasswell family from Boston. They had it for some years in the parlor of their brownstone on Commonwealth Avenue. They specified in their wills that it be given to the South Shore Historical Society. From what I gather the Historical Society didn't want it. . . well, to put it nicely didn't have a place for it . . . so sold it to an auction house on the Cape which is where the Snodgrass's bid on it and picked it up. I'm going to figure out how to get that bastard Crankshaw to give back to our family his ill-gotten gains. Tomorrow I'm meeting with Ed Friendly at his office in Boston to find out how we go about it legally."

"Oh for God sakes, Ted, give it a rest. You're making yourself sick. Nobody in the family wants or needs the money and surely you don't want to pull the rug out from under the feet of Snodgrass."

"Well I want to do something to get that son of a bitch Crankshaw. To get him out of this town and to put a stop to the way he's preying on fine old families who've worked hard all their lives. I want him exposed before he bilks any others out of the inheritance they're due."

"Sorry to have to tell you this darling but Priscilla is extremely happy in her life with Crankshaw. Word is that he has moved in for good, not just for the few weeks to get her settled."

"But this should not be allowed! Surely

Parker must object. His wife has dementia and this young buck moves in and lives off her money – their money."

"They say he has his own money and is sharing expenses. Apparently they are very much in love."

"Bullshit. He should be locked up."

"I'm going to bring lunch out. It'll be good to sit in the sun. Read your book while you wait."

"I've never felt like this before Priscilla. You are so beautiful inside and out. I can't stop thinking about you."

"But I'm old, slow, and wrinkly."

"You are not. I love being with you. I can't take my eyes off you."

Loring Crankshaw and Priscilla Tappertit had settled into a comfortable routine. Ocean

View Acres accepted the set up. Having Crankshaw living in with Priscilla cut back on the work that ordinarily would be assigned to one of the nurses' aides or caregivers hired by the assisted living facility. Parker was charged the minimum rate for his wife – the one meal per day plan – which they rarely ate in the dining room.

"I have to tell you I am very much in love with you," Crankshaw said to Priscilla. "It seems we can talk for hours and we have so much in common." They looked at each other across the small dining table at the end of the living room as they finished a lobster casserole.

"I feel badly leaving Parker."

"You're not exactly leaving Parker. Seems to me he's left you."

"I guess you're right. But we were happily

married for fifty-five years, though I was difficult and especially these last three or four
years."

"Let's just see how it goes for a few more
days. I would love to stay with you, to live
with you. But I don't want people to think I'm
after your money."

The phone rang. Loring left the table and
picked up the receiver in the bedroom. It was
Parker telling him he had to return to Ontario
the following week. He would like to pay him
and talk with him about Priscilla and her life
at Ocean View. He suggested lunch the next
day.

Crankshaw told Priscilla and talked more
about their situation. She was disturbed,
feeling sure this would not be acceptable to
Parker and the family.

"Come here," Loring called to her. "Sit on the couch with me and let me hold you in my arms. I love you and will do anything to help you through this. I think it will all work out for the best. Your family sees that you are much better. I've never seen anything wrong with you. May I sleep with you tonight – no hanky panky. Just let me in your bed to be there for you and you for me in the night to give comfort."

Loring Crankshaw had stayed in Ocean View Acres for over a month. By now Parker and the rest of the family have been to visit Priscilla. Loring made himself scarce during their visits. Parker was delighted to see that his wife had settled in comfortably and didn't seem to care that he was not there with her. She was glowing and Parker was pleased he'd made the right choice. He didn't question Crankshaw's motives and was glad it was working for Priscilla. He'd had difficult years with her when she was depressed or angry. He didn't know how to handle her and spent more and more time away, having hired a series of caretakers.

He'd moved into the Big House or into one of the rooms in one house or another in the Compound as the summer wore on. He bunked in with Dorothy one night when she was frightened of the lightening, got a little drunk and suggested he stay in the spare room. He made a few asides saying that he might be able to offer more comfort if he slept with her, but she would have none of it that night. Later, though, they slipped into a comfortable arrangement and for all intents and purposes, he moved in to the guest house with her. He was planning to move back to Ontario in September and Dorothy would go with him. The blueberry crop beckoned he told her.

Parker called Ted and asked him to meet him and Crankshaw for coffee downtown.

Eleven

They were waiting for Crankshaw in the Plymouth Rock Clam Shack overlooking the harbor. Ted was telling Parker about Crankshaw and his reputation.

"He's probably taken some of your stuff. I'm sorry I didn't have the chance to warn you. I mentioned it to Dorothy but apparently she didn't take it seriously. I've followed the provenance of one of the rugs that was in my grandmother's house. Apparently Crankshaw made a killing on it; it was one of his 'investments'. I'm talking to my lawyer tomorrow to see what I can do about it. I've met with other families who've used Crankshaw. Even if I can't get reparations in some form, I want to get this scam out in the public so no other families are bilked. He's got a crafty little business going. Even if someone might have suspicions, most families are so happy with the work he does they don't care if he swipes a few little things."

"So why bother," Parker asked.

"Because it's stealing. People should not get away with stealing when they are given such trust. What if when you go back to your house in Canada you find stuff not there?"

"Well, I guess I wouldn't know if a silver bowl or some old bibelot was gone. Either I wouldn't know, or would assume it's at Priscilla's apartment here at Ocean View."

"Exactly. This happened to my family. I think a lot of my grandparent's treasured pieces are gone but everyone thought one of the other family members had them. Another reason I bring this up is that Crankshaw appears to have moved in with your wife."

"I know. He's staying on to help her settle in. It's a comfortable arrangement. He apparently is there until his next job opens up. She's never looked happier. She always had some problems with my family that I never understood. Crankshaw worships her and she knows it."

"But doesn't that bother you? For one thing living on her money—your money—and for another thing, aren't you jealous?"

"Let her have her day—her last days. Actually I think Crankshaw really loves her.

His father was an artist, you know, and he understands her temperament. Frankly she was not an easy woman to live with, or I should say for me to live with. Very uptight in public, trying to live up to her idea of what a judge's wife should look like and then morose and depressed at home. The children and I have always loved summer life in the Plymouth Compound. She hated it. She did better on the farm in Canada, but still it was not easy. I guess she really didn't like me or my ways. Of course I couldn't divorce her. She was in pretty bad shape and even spent time at a psychiatric hospital. Electric shock therapy helped but didn't cure. Loring Crankshaw loves her. I say let them be.

"Sorry Parker. I didn't know all this. I'll have to reconsider my plan. I don't want to hurt you and Priscilla and your family. But I also don't want this kind of thing going on without some light on the crime. Thanks for explaining and I'll try to stay in control when he gets here."

Loring Crankshaw found Ted and Parker at a window table in the Clam Shack. They stood. Parker introduced Ted to Loring, they shook hands all around and sat. "The chowder here is the best on the south shore—at least it's voted the best, year after year in the local newspaper. Will you join us for a Bloody Mary or Cape Codder first?"

They put in their order and made small talk. "I asked you here to talk about Priscilla," said Parker. "First of all, thank you for making the move comfortable for her and for all of us. I want to talk about your charges and her future.

Secondly, I want to introduce you again to Ted Brooks. He is a member of the family of one of your first clients. He was not there when the family house was broken up in East Middletown nor when the surviving daughter, Harriet, Ted's aunt, died. Ted was in the Foreign Service, living abroad during those years.'

"Oh yes," said Loring, "of course I remember your family. Your . . . would it be grandmother? . . . was a good friend of my father and an early supporter of his art. She bought many of his paintings."

"Yes," Ted interrupted. "Well I came across a rug of hers right here in downtown Plymouth and I just want an explanation. I've talked to some of your so-called clients and I know you've been bilking people right and left."

"Wait a minute," Parker interrupted. "We don't know this. Calm down Ted."

"It's pretty clear what your game is, Crankshaw, and it's time we put a halt to it. You should not keep preying on the old and demented population."

Loring said nothing.

Ted stood and started pacing the aisles of the restaurant. He went to the window, looked out over the terrace to the ocean beyond. He was frenzied, pounded one hand into the other, his hair was disheveled, and sweat was pouring down the side of his face.

Loring and Parker sat in silent embarrassment.

"Let's discuss your charges," Parker said to Loring, "and how you see Priscilla's future.

I'm going back to Canada next week. How do you think she'll cope?"

"I think she's doing fine. I'd like to stay on for a while if that's all right with you. We're comfortable with each other."

"What do you mean by that?"

"I'm helping her settle in. We're compatible and have a lot in common. She knows of my father, the artist, and is an admirer. Well, to be honest I love her. I love her very much and I believe she loves me."

CPSIA information can be obtained
at www.ICGtesting.com
Printed in the USA
LVHW111128251120
672638LV00006B/514